The Iris

The flowers on the cover of this book are named for the ancient Greek goddess of the rainbow and messenger of the gods, Iris. It is said that Iris had the ability to connect heaven and earth with a beautiful rainbow, allowing the gods to communicate with mankind. Like Iris' rainbow, books are our vechicle of communication, connecting us to new ideas, transporting us to amazing places and helping us to gain insight, understanding and knowledge. We at Half Price Books would like to encourage readers and writers of all ages to continue to create, to dream, to learn and to grow.

About this Book

Half Price Books has been supporting literacy since its founding in 1972. Eight years ago, we sponsored our first Bedtime Storybook Contest, open to amateur writers of all ages. Through the years we have received entries from some of the most talented, undiscovered writers in the country. Each year the Bedtime Storybook Contest is greeted with great enthusiasm. We appreciate our customers' continued support of this contest, and would like to thank the writers, illustrators and judges for their time and dedication. Next year's entry forms for this contest will be available at all Half Price Books locations beginning January 1.

Special thanks to Irena Roman, Professor at the Massachusetts College of Art, for her cover illustration.

Say Good Night
to Illiteracy

8th Edition

Table of Contents

Big Frog, Little Frog

Big Frog, Little Frog
Feet on a log,
Sunset, moon met
Water in the bog.

Said Little Frog to Big Frog,
With crickets creaking loud,
"What are lights, bright sights
Peeking through the clouds?"

Said Big Frog to Little Frog,
Croaking in reply,
"Fireflies, flown too high,
Stuck in the sky."

Said Little Frog to Big Frog,
Now nervous indeed,
"Why does wind whistle, bend thistle
And rustle through the reed?"

Said Big Frog to Little Frog,
Swaying with the breeze,
"It's nothing more than Sun's snore
And Moon's gentle sneeze."

Said Little Frog to Big Frog,
While clouds clamor on,
"Why does rain drop, plink and plop
And play upon our pond?"

Said Big Frog to Little Frog,
Smiling to the sky,
"It's night's song, soft and long—
A little frog's lullaby."

Big Frog, Croaking Frog,
Little Frog in dream land.
Little Frog, Happy Frog,
With Daddy Frog at hand.

—Paul Cummings
Computer Technician

The Gardener

My mother was born with a very green thumb.
She grew corn up to the sky when I was young.

She used her clever grafting ability
To grow three kinds of **apples** on one single tree.

But her true forte was not **vegetables** and **fruit**:
It was her flower gardens — grown from seed, root and shoot.

She grew a **blue hydrangea** as tall as me,
At the corner of the house, near the **red Hawthorn tree**.

In the first breath of spring, the first bloom we saw
Was the bright yellow forsythia, against the fence wall.

Soon after were **tulips** and **bluebells** and camellias
Then came **lilacs** and **irises** and bright pink azaleas.

My mom would gather them up in **colorful** arrays.
The whole house was filled with the scent of bouquets.

Clematis entwined into high-climbing **roses**,
Asters and daisies, **lilies** and **posies**.

All summer long they paraded into view:
Dahlias, **carnations**, **peonies** and even fescue.

In the fall, just as things began to be humdrum,
Came the last of the flowers — orange chrysanthemums.

She gardens still and when I visit she places
Flowers in the guest bedroom in pretty crystal vases.

— Sandra Walker
Development Director

When I travel to the amusement park
My favorite ride of all,
Is the giant roller coaster.
It's so big and very tall.

I enter through the waiting line
And hop in the front car.
The attendant helps fasten me in
With the wide lap bar.

The car pulls out of the station
And begins to climb the track.
I sit and wait anxiously
Listening to the clickety clack.

I look down and wave to friends below
And when I reach the top,
I brace myself with excitement
As the car begins to drop.

I let out a scream of delight
As we free-fall down the hill.
The car quickly accelerates
Giving me a thrill.

We pass through a loop.
We roar through a tunnel.
We twirl around a helix
That's shaped like a funnel.

The car returns to the station
And then the ride ends.
I run back in line
To do it all over again!

—Jordan Smith
6th Grade Student

13

My shoes and socks don't get along

I jumped from bed and grabbed my sword.
Saturday! No school! I could explore!

Treasure and new land I'd discover.
"Not so fast," said my Mother.

"Before you venture into the wild,
You must clean your room, my dear child."

True, my room was in a state,
But my adventure could not wait.

"I cannot hide what's going on.
My shoes and socks don't get along.

"They toss, and turn, and roll around
Like wrestling boys without a sound.

"My clothes are happy in a pile.
They need to rest for just awhile.

"They can't relax or take a break
On wire hangers that are so straight.

"My blankets lie crumpled on the bed.
'There'll be no folding,' is what they said.

"They might look soft and warm to you,
But blankets can be vicious too.

"I know my toys lay strewn about.
They begged and begged to be let out.

"Their big toy box is dark and scary,
Full of monsters, mean and hairy.

My mom was quite amazed to hear
Of all the chaos that was so near.

"You must regain your fading power.
This room is fierce, don't be a coward.

"When your socks and shoes begin to fight,
There's one thing you do to set them right.

"Take your socks and fold them flat
And place your shoes upon the mat.

"If your pants and shirts begin to whine,
Just remember to say this line,

'Clothes should hang neat and pressed
So I can always look my best.'

"Every morning when you wake,
Your crumpled bed you shall make.

"If that blanket growls at you,
Tell him that you know kung fu.

"Your small toys have more to fear
Than a dark box where beasts may leer.

"A foot may crush your favorite toy
And leave you sad, my dear boy.

"This room is yours to care for son.
When it's neat, you'll have more fun.

"I know that you are strong and smart,
I'll be glad to help you make a start."

—Amy L. Woods
Merchandise Representative

15

The Spider

That Frightened Miss Muffet Away

When Little Miss Muffet sat on her tuffet, eating her curds and whey,
I wonder what kind of spider she saw on that particular day.

Perhaps it was the black widow spider, on its bottom it has a red mark,
It prefers garages, basements, attics and places that are dark.

Or maybe it was the giant tarantula who eats frogs, lizards and snakes.
He may have wanted to join Miss Muffet in her dinner of curds and whey.

It could have been the jumping spider, the best jumper of all.
It can jump over forty times its length and is extremely small.

Maybe if Little Miss Muffet knew more about these particular spiders,
She might have thought it a compliment that one would want to sit beside her.

–Cameron Smith
4th Grade Student

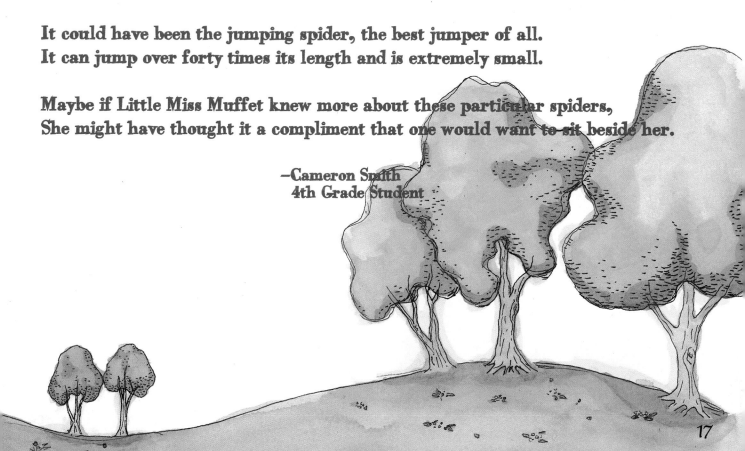

17

LUCY AND BRIDGET'S LONG JOURNEY

I'm Ladybug Lucy, please come with me
And my friend Bridget, a nice bumblebee.
On delicate dainty wings we will fly,
Far, far away, up in the sky.
We'll put on our goggles and baseball caps,
Bring our passports, a suitcase and several world maps.

The first stop of our magnificent journey will be
A nice little jaunt to see Germany,
Watch fussball*, tour a castle and eat chocolate cake.
And now onto the next stop we will make.

We're flying over the Mediterranean Sea—
The Leaning Tower of Pisa—we're in Italy!
Let's ride a gondola, see Mt. Vesuvius too.
Now we're off again, there's so much to do!

Soon we're in France, berets snugly in place,
In the Tour de France, the bicycle race.
Oh look we see the Eiffel Tower afar.
But it's time to go, we say au revoir.

We'll travel to England, Windsor Castle we'll see,
And dine on crumpets with a warm spot of tea,
Watch the Changing of the Guard and hear Big Ben,
Visit Trafalgar Square, Kew Gardens and then…

It's time to go home, our journey must end.
We're glad you could join us, our new little friend.
We have traveled the world, both far and wide—
To our beds we must go, tucked safely inside!

–Rhonda Bleska & Rena Shaw
Mother & Daughter

*In Germany, soccer is called fussball.

My Island

On my island, dolphins play.

On my island, I have my own way.

On my island, winter is cold.

On my island, summer's gold.

On my island, days are peaceful.

On my island, nights are gleeful.

On my island, lives one soul.

On my island, life has a toll.

My island is here, through good and bad.

Sometimes on my island, I feel sad.

On my island, flowers bloom.

Where is my island? Right in my room.

—Erica Madore
6th Grade Student

Beware the giant monster,
Who lives inside the lake.
In spite of what you may have heard,
This monster is no fake.

What this giant monster is,
We really cannot say.
Did it come from our forgotten past,
Or some place far away?

Sometimes on dark and lonely nights,
The monster comes on shore.
We'll find its footprints on the beach,
And hear its frightful roar.

A friend of mine once saw the beast,
When he went out for a swim.
He heard this very loud splashing sound,
As the beast came after him.

He barely got to shore in time,
And the thought still makes him shake.
The water was all foamy,
From the monster's giant wake.

No one's ever photographed this beast—
Attempts to catch it fail.
Small boats are smashed or capsized
By the monster's giant tail.

There's talk of myths and magic,
Or things from outer space.
But no one really knows for sure
About this haunted place.

So beware this giant monster
With its evil scary groans.
For if you don't you may become,
A pile of chewed up bones.

—Jay Berkowitz
Art Teacher

The 1939 New York World's Fair

That wondrous place, the New York World's Fair, is alive and well in my memory. It was 1939 and, for a six-year-old, it held every fascinating and exciting adventure. Way beyond today's television and movies... This was in the fresh air, with the smells and sounds of another world, the rush of people and the hum of movement.

I raised my eyes to the Trylon and Perisphere, higher, higher and STILL I had to look UP. The buildings were so white, dazzling, and the people who walked on the ramps were tiny. Were they real PEOPLE?

There was music and rhythm and smells of delectable foods. We had dressed up for this event, even with all the walking and running and eating and climbing. No jeans and sneakers. We wore Mary Janes on our feet and dotted swiss dresses and our hair was ribboned.

At the Odditorium, everything was bigger, and smaller, and stranger. There were even babies to see, the Dionne quintuplets—that miraculous event. FIVE babies! This was even more than our cat Mitzi had at one time.

But best of all was the parachute ride. I grabbed my sister's hand, and we were buckled in the seat. We began to rise, swaying in the seat, terrified, TERRIFIED, and below us was THE WORLD. The world as we knew it and more of the skyline of New York than we had ever seen, swaying there for a LONG TIME...then we were lowered, gliding and the parachute, red and billowy, opened above to take us back to earth. We had been to the heavens and had returned, braver than ever on our shaky knees. This was the 1939 New York World's Fair.

—Lori Gelzer
Retired

27

The sky was blue with polka dot clouds
When Jennifer Lee went walking.
She came upon a very tall man
Who hunched to hear her talking.

Pardon me," said Jennifer Lee, "but how do you tie your shoes?"

I have a friend," the tall man said,
Who lives in the house next door.
He kindly helps; he's rather short,
He measures 3 foot 4."

Jennifer Lee went down to the park
And sat by the children's swings.
She saw a boy swing over the top.
She marveled at such a thing.

Pardon me," said Jennifer Lee, "but how did you swing around?"

I learned from my dad," the young boy said.
He learned from his dad before.
My grandpa, you see, was an acrobat,
He knew how to swing and soar."

Jennifer Lee walked on to the zoo
And purchased a ticket for one.
She hurried along to the penguins' pond.
She found them such jolly fun.

Pardon me," said Jennifer Lee, "but why do you stand in a row?"

The penguins laughed and shivered their wings.
It's just what penguins do.
We look so elegant, don't you think,
And perfectly handsome, too."

Jennifer Lee sat under a tree
And looked at a crooked bough.
A robin was packing his suitcase there.
Well, why was he leaving now?

"Pardon me," said Jennifer Lee, "but where are you traveling to?"

"The winter is coming soon, you know,
And southbound we must fly.
I'm taking my favorite bathing suit,"
The robin said. "Good-bye!"

Jennifer Lee walked all the way home,
And made a cup of tea.
The world was an interesting place, she thought,
Tomorrow, what will I see?

—Mercedes Lawry
Director of Media & Public Relations

29

At the Market

Dirty farm hands,
Drab overalls
And crinkled tan faces
At the booths
Selling fresh peaches,
Firm bright tomatoes
And homemade blackberry jam.

We fill our trunk
Then smell the sweetness riding home.
We all spend the afternoon
Peeling and slicing peaches to freeze,
Eating sliced tomatoes sprinkled with salt
And making biscuits for tasting the jam.

At sundown,
The farmers load
The produce trucks
And journey home.

— Natallia Jones
Legal Secretary

Bibliography Banks

There once was a girl, Miss Banks was her name,
Who got the idea that she was too plain.
Her look was pretty, her clothing the same,
Mostly she suffered 'cause her name was just Jane.

She wanted a name you would find in a book.
One like Rapunzel that had a great hook.
Cinderella, Snow White, Belle and Nanook,
They had the right ring, but Jane hadn't the look.

Jane had been Jane forever and a day.
In fact she turned 8 years old this past May.
Off to the library for a name that would fit.
Jane found a crowd and nowhere to sit.

Behind the front desk Jane saw a free chair.
Would the librarian mind, or even care,
If Jane sat for a while at this vacant perch?
She had books to look at and names to research!

Jane's armful of books was the storybook kind,
Where powerful names shouldn't be hard to find.
Turning page by page searching cover to cover,
A name that was fitting she hoped to discover.

She read every word that made up every sentence.
Then—there it was—
"The New York Public Library Desk Reference."

This is the book with the most information—
Dates, names and lists in such concentration.
An awesome big book meant for librarian use.
Jane couldn't resist; she'll make no excuse.

The reading was hard, the words most intense,
Like Index, Preface and Table of Contents.
She found the name herself, to Jane goes the thanks,
and tomorrow she'll be Bibliography Banks.

—Andrea Z. Jensen
English Teacher

Spaghetti Lucia

1 package of spaghetti
1 jar of your favorite spaghetti sauce

Heat a big pot of water until it boils.
Put in the spaghetti and cook until it is soft
but not mushy (about 7 minutes).

Drain the spaghetti to get out all the water.
Put the sauce into the pot with the spaghetti,
stir, and heat until it is warm enough to eat.

Sprinkle on cheese if you like, and serve.

34

Mama Mia, It's Lucia!

In a little town called Bloomingdale,
Where purple tulips grow,
There lives a very special cat,
I'd like you all to know.

This cat has fur as black as night,
With eyes so golden green—
A narrow streak of pure white fur,
Under her neck can be seen.

What make this feline special,
So different from the rest,
Is that this cat can really cook—
Her spaghetti is the best!

How this animal learned to cook,
No one really knows.
When cooking, she wears a purple apron
Cooking while standing on her toes.

All the ladies and men in town,
All of the girls and boys too,
Love to visit her purple kitchen
While she's making something new.

This cat is kind to people.
She cooks for everyone in town.
If you ever feel lonely or sad,
Her cooking will erase your frown.

When the townspeople ate the cat's spaghetti,
They all shouted Mama Mia!
Their tummies were full and happy,
All because of a cat named Lucia.

—Keleigh Sinclaire
Business Owner

When you can't rest
They say it's best
To count sheep in your head.
But what if sheep
Can't fall asleep
When it's time to go to bed?

Sheep can't count sheep
To get to sleep
For that would just be strange.
No, other sights
Must fill the nights
And occupy their brains.

Perhaps it's bunnies
Wearing undies
While dancing Irish jigs.
Or maybe toucans
Knitting afghans
For each of their pet pigs.

Now, panda bears
With long nose hairs
Are fun to count at night.
Just like mosquitoes
Wearing speedos
(As long as they don't bite).

It may be dogs
In wooden clogs
Slurping noodles through a straw.
Or could it be
It's you and me
The sheep are counting...NAW!

Sheep can't count sheep
To go to sleep
For that would just be strange.
It's better though
That we don't know
What occupies their brains!

—Stacy A. Hillmer
12th Grade Student

37

Seashore Harmony

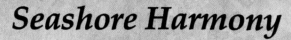

When Lizzy and I went down to the sea,
The sun shone all day in the sky.
We waded in water with fluffy sea foam
And listened to white sea gulls' cry.

Out crawled a crab from a hole in the sand.
It scuttled away in a flash.
While out past the breakers swam silvery fish
That leaped and then dove with a splash.

We jumped in the waves holding hands very tight,
Then floated and looked at the sky,
At puffy white clouds just like seabirds in flight,
So soft as they swiftly sailed by.

Then, we played in the dunes in the warm afternoon
And saw tiny footprints all around
That led to small burrows in long, waving grass,
Where the beach creatures live, safe and sound.

Then, back to the shore with the waves rolling in,
We ran with a shout of delight.
The sand crabs all scuttled back into their holes.
We nearly could touch them—but not quite.

As the red-orange sun sank low in the sky
And the blue sea turned slowly to gold,
We waved to the waves and we said our goodbye,
And we happily headed for home.

—Pauline & Vincent Forbes
Husband & Wife

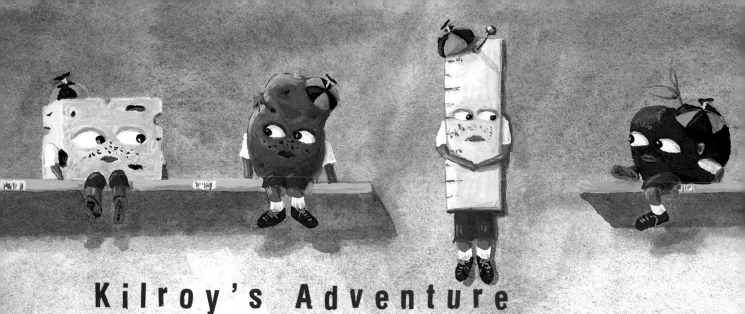

Kilroy's Adventure

One day, while at the local grocery store, little Kilroy's mommy left without him. The grocer thought he was cheese so he put Kilroy on the deli shelf.

A woman then came in thinking he was cheese so she bought him. Then, she noticed her cheese had eyes. "Eyes!" she said, "This must be a potato." So she took the 'potato' back to the grocers.

Then, a doctor bought Kilroy and was about to french-fry him when he noticed his potato had feet. "Feet!" the doctor exclaimed, "This must be a ruler." So he took the 'ruler' back to the grocers.

Next, a teacher was looking at art supplies and noticed one of the rulers had skin. "This can't be a ruler," she said. "If it has skin, it must be an apple!" So she put the 'apple' in the produce section.

Next, a hungry mailman purchased Kilroy. He was just about to peel him, when he saw an ear on his apple! "If this fruit has an ear," he thought, "it must be corn." Back to the grocers he took the 'corn.'

A lawyer bought Kilroy along with other ears of corn. She was just going to cook them up when she saw one of her ears of corn had a neck. "Well bottles have necks, but corn doesn't," she said. So she took the 'soda bottle' back to the grocers.

A thirsty policeman bought a cola, which happened to be Kilroy. He was getting ready to open it when he observed a leg. "A leg!" he thought. "This can't be soda. If it has a leg, it must be a table."

After Kilroy was back at the store, the grocer started to set up a display on him. At that moment, a lady busted in and said to the grocer, "Stop! He is way too warm and sweet to be a table!"

"Warm and sweet?" said the confused grocer. "Then, Ma'am, that must be a pie."

"Pie, my eye—If that's a pie," said the woman, "then, I'm a pie, too!"

Then Kilroy and his mommy went home.

—Benjamin Gore
9th Grade Student

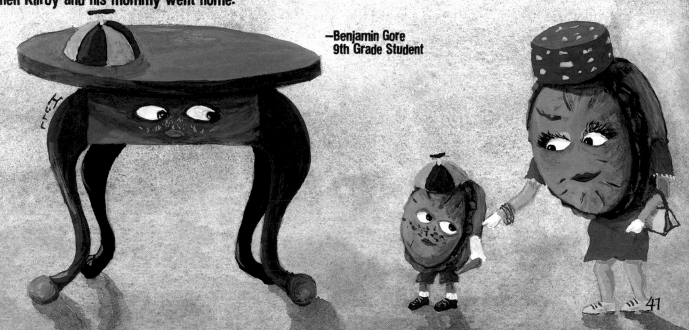

41

Harry was just a regular, average kid. He had just awoken and was in the kitchen pouring himself a glass of milk. His sister, Nancy, came down the stairs into the kitchen. "Morning," she said.

"Hi, sis," he mumbled back. Then, Nancy picked up a package of bagels and reached for the toaster, when she accidentally knocked over the milk and spilled it.

She slipped, and the bagels flew out the open window and hit the postman in the face. His mailbag fell and split open, scattering mail everywhere. A particularly large envelope flew right in front of a car's windshield and blocked the driver's view of the road.

The driver turned the wheel to the left and splashed mud on a man riding a bicycle. The man got mud in his eyes and almost hit a woman that was carrying boxes. The startled woman flung her arms up and the boxes flew everywhere. One box hit a beehive in a tree.

The angry bees flew toward a girl that was playing hop-scotch nearby. She started to run and knocked over a painter's ladder, splashing paint on a girl riding on her scooter. She ran into a rosebush that a gardener was pruning. The gardener dodged the girl but accidentally stepped on his cat's tail. The cat zoomed into the middle of the street and ran right in front of a school bus.

By now, Harry and Nancy were on this bus on their way to school. The bus driver hit the brakes hard, missing the cat, but causing all of the kids to bump their heads on the seat in front of them.

The moral of this story: A little mistake can later hit you on the head.

—Justin Arredondo-Guerrero
5th Grade Student

44

The Moon Watches

The moon watches over the dark plains of Africa. Vingi, the elephant calf sees it, and thinks it is a huge elephant tusk guarding the night. It makes him feel safe. He snuggles beside his mother and she wraps her trunk around him. He goes to sleep.
The moon watches.

Mitti, the giraffe calf sees it, and thinks it is a giant silver leaf. When her neck grows long enough she will pick it. She presses close to her mother's side, flicks her tail, and dreams of eating the juiciest leaf in the world.
The moon watches.

Doobie, the zebra foal sees it, and thinks it is the brightest zebra stripe of all. When he is big he will run faster than all other zebras, and catch the stripe and wear it. He stamps his hooves and blows through his nostrils, just to show how big he is getting already. Then he settles close to his mother, tucking his hooves under him.
The moon watches.

Vooboo, the hippo calf sees it, and thinks it is a pool just the right size for her. She stares longingly at it and wishes it would come down and let her splash in it. Then she follows her mother on the long night's walk in search of food.
The moon watches.

Thulani, the game ranger's son, gazes at the moon gleaming outside his window. Sometimes he thinks it is a huge diamond. Maybe he will climb the stars to fetch it down and make it into a necklace for his mother. But he knows it is really the moon watching over the plains of Africa. His mother tucks him into bed and he says, "Good night, moon."

But the moon does not run or splash or sleep or dream or answer.
The moon watches.

—Avil Vandermerwe
Retired

RAY-MEL CORNELIUS

43

Authors

Big Frog, Little Frog (Third Place Winner)	Paul Cummings	Austin, TX
The Gardener	Sandra Walker	Dallas, TX
How Kittens Got Their Meow	Gina Zanella	Snoqualmie, WA
Roller Coaster Ride	Jordan Smith	Fort Worth, TX
My Shoes & Socks Don't Get Along	Amy L. Woods	San Antonio, TX
The Spider That Frightened Miss Muffet Away	Cameron Smith	Fort Worth, TX
Lucy & Bridget's Long Journey	Rhonda Bleska & Rena Shaw	West Chester & Miamisburg, OH
My Island	Erica Madore	Apple Valley, MN
Three Sisters	Dolores Kleinholz	Edmonds, WA
The Giant Monster	Jay Berkowitz	Lyndhurst, OH
The 1939 New York World's Fair	Lori L. Gelzer	Mercer Island, WA
Pardon Me	Mercedes Lawry	Seattle, WA
At the Market	Natallia P. Jones	Fort Worth, TX
Bibliography Banks	Andrea Jensen	Grapevine, TX
Mama Mia, It's Lucia	Keleigh Sinclaire	Arlington, TX
When Sheep Can't Sleep (Second Place Winner)	Stacy Hillmer	Waukesha, WI
Seashore Harmony	Pauline & Vincent Forbes	San Antonio, TX
Kilroy's Adventure	Benjamin Gore	Snoqualmie, WA
Don't Spill the Milk	Justin Arredondo-Guerrero	San Antonio, TX
The Moon Watches (Grand Prize Winner)	Avil Vandermerwe	Edmonds, WA

Illustrators

Guillermo Becerra · Bonnie Bonnevie · Jim Brooks · Ray-Mel Cornelius · Julia "Fitzy" Fitzmaurice · Eric Granados
Maiko Hamaaki · Martha Hull · Patt Kelley · Lana McFattridge · Nicole Melino · Mamiko Ohashi
Cielo Oreste · Hye Yun Park · Amy Patacchiola · Chet Phillips · Irena Roman · Ingrid Sundberg · Ellen Tanner · Julie York

We hope you have enjoyed the 8th Edition of the Half Price Books Bedtime Storybook. Because of our continuing commitment to literacy, proceeds from sales of this book will be donated to the following literacy groups:

Cleveland Reads
Corpus Christi Literacy Council
Dallas Reads
DMACC Adult Literacy
Greater Milwaukee Literacy Coalition
Greater Pittsburgh Literacy Council
Houston READ Commission
Indiana Literacy Foundation
Indianapolis Adult Literacy Coalition
King County Library System
Literacy Austin
The Literacy Initiative
Literacy Instruction For Texas (LIFT)
Literacy Network of Greater Cincinnati
Literacy Volunteers of Maricopa County, Inc.
LVA-Brazos Valley
Madison Literacy Council
Metropolitan Alliance for Adult Learning
Minnesota Literacy Council
National Alliance of Urban Literacy Coalition
Project READ
Project Second Chance
San Antonio Commission on Literacy
Score a Goal in the Classroom
St. Paul Reads
Washington Literacy

Each year the Bedtime Storybook Contest is greeted with great enthusiasm. We appreciate our customers' continued support of this project, and would like to thank the writers, judges and illustrators for their time and dedication to this book. For more information about this project, or any of our literacy endeavors, or to purchase additional copies of this book, visit our web site at www.halfpricebooks.com.

ISBN 1-9310-4016-8

Kelly Press
10 Hitt Street
Columbia, Missouri 65205
573/449-4163

Printed on recycled paper.